THE LITTLE PRINCESS

THE LITTLE PRINCESS

MAPLE SPRING PUBLISHING

Published 2024 by Maple Spring Publishing

Front cover design by David Rheinhardt of Pyrographx
Interior design by Jason Snyder

Library of Congress Cataloging-in-Publication Data is available upon request

ISBN: 979-8-3505-0116-2

10 9 8 7 6 5 4 3 2 1

CAST

Shirley Temple . . . . .Sara Crewe

Richard Greene . . . . Geoffrey Hamilton

Anita Louise. . . . . .Rose

Ian Hunter . . . . Captain Reginald Crewe

Cesar Romero. . . . . .Ram Dass

Arthur Treacher . . . . .Hubert "Bertie" Minchin

Mary Nash . . . . Mistress Amanda Minchin

Sybil Jason. . . . . .Becky

Miles Mander . . . . .Lord Wickham

Marcia Mae Jones . . . . .Lavinia

Deidre Gale. . . . . Jessie

Ira Stevens . . . . .Ermengarde

E.E. Clive . . . . .Mr. Barrows

Beryl Mercer. . . . . .Queen Victoria

Eily Malyon . . . . .Mrs. O'Connell the Cook

Rita Paige . . . . Minnie the Cook's Helper

Lionel Braham . . . . .Colonel Gordon

ENGLAND, 1899. We see a panorama of the great sights of London: London Bridge, the Tower, a beefeater in a bear-skin shako marching back and forth. And a majestic portrait of Queen Victoria.

Then we see soldiers marching and a newspaper headline: "Boers Threaten WAR! Regiment Departs for the Transvaal." A crowd, watching them march past, is waving and applauding.

Sara Crewe and her father, Captain Reginald Crewe, are watching the parade from a window.

SARA CREWE

Why are they sending so many soldiers, Daddy, if it's only going to be a little war?

CAPTAIN REGINALD CREWE

Make those stubborn Boers take us seriously this time, my darling. They'll realize Her Majesty intends to put a stop to their nonsense. They'll quiet down.

SARA CREWE

They'd better. Anyhow, when you get there, you'll stop them, won't you, Daddy?

CAPTAIN REGINALD CREWE

I do my best, dear.

A crowded street scene. Captain Crewe and Sara are riding in a carriage.

SARA CREWE

I'm going to miss you so.

CAPTAIN REGINALD CREWE

I'll be back, and we'll be together again, before you can say "knife."

SARA CREWE

I can say "knife" a good many times in a year.

CAPTAIN REGINALD CREWE

At the school, you'll have charming little girls to play with, books to read, a pony to ride. And after all, there'll be Emily, you know?

SARA CREWE

Yes, there will be Emily *(her doll)*. And she does look as though should be an understanding friend. Don't you think, daddy?

CAPTAIN REGINALD CREWE

With that intellectual forehead, I'm sure of it.

They approach a building with a brass plate: "Miss Minchin's Seminary."

SARA CREWE

It's not a very cheerful looking school, is it, Daddy?

CAPTAIN REGINALD CREWE

I'm afraid nothing will seem very cheerful to us at the moment.

SARA CREWE

Well, maybe it'll be better on the inside.

CAPTAIN REGINALD CREWE

Of course it will.

At the front door, a groom is leading a struggling pony out. Mistress Amanda Minchin and her brother, Hubert "Bertie" Minchin, are behind.

CAPTAIN CREWE

Oh, I say! Just a moment!

GROOM

I'm sorry, sir.

HUBERT "BERTIE" MINCHIN

Sorry. We're all sorry. Get it out.

MISTRESS AMANDA MINCHIN

The very idea of delivering a thing like this at the front door!

SARA CREWE

Oh, look, daddy, my pony!

MISTRESS AMANDA MINCHIN

(to the groom)

Your employer will answer for this. Now take him away.

HUBERT "BERTIE" MINCHIN

Yes, far away.

SARA CREWE

Oh no, daddy.

Captain Crewe goes up the steps to Miss Minchin and Bertie.

CAPTAIN REGINALD CREWE

Oh, I say, just a moment. You are Miss Minchin?

MISTRESS AMANDA MINCHIN

I am.

CAPTAIN REGINALD CREWE

I'm Captain Crewe. I'm afraid I've caused you no end of inconvenience.

MISTRESS AMANDA MINCHIN

You most certainly have, Captain Crewe.

CAPTAIN REGINALD CREWE

May I step inside and explain?

MISTRESS AMANDA MINCHIN

Come in.

CAPTAIN REGINALD CREWE

Wait here with the pony.

GROOM

Righto, governor.

They go inside the building.

CAPTAIN REGINALD CREWE

I'm terribly sorry. I had no intention of having the pony delivered inside your house.

MISTRESS AMANDA MINCHIN

There are a number of things beside the pony. Parcels have been arriving here, collect, for your daughter for hours. Follow me, please.

They go into Miss Minchin's study. As they pass, Becky, a little girl in a very dingy outfit, is shining ladies' boots. She looks up longingly at them.

Mistress Minchin is seated at her desk in her study, Captain Crewe and Sara seated in front of it, Bertie standing over them.

MISTRESS MINCHIN

Apparently, you are not aware, Captain Crewe, that I conduct one of the most dignified and exclusive schools in London.

CAPTAIN REGINALD CREWE

Oh, yes, yes, so I understood. That's precisely the reason why I brought my daughter to you.

MISTRESS AMANDA MINCHIN

I would not have gathered that from your actions.

CAPTAIN REGINALD CREWE

Really now, I'm not entirely to blame. You see, Sara and I have only just arrived from India. Sara's lived there practically all her life. We'd no more than got here when I learned that my regiment was to leave at once for South Africa, so we had to act hurriedly.

MISTRESS AMANDA MINCHIN

But I wrote you explaining that I do not take young ladies without an interview and the most impeccable references. I wrote you also that at the moment I had no vacant rooms.

SARA CREWE

Well, in that case, Daddy, we might as well move on.

CAPTAIN REGINALD CREWE

This is a bit awkward. You see, your letter never reached me. And I'm afraid it never occurred to me that any school wouldn't welcome my little Sara.

MISTRESS AMANDA MINCHIN

Obviously.

CAPTAIN REGINALD CREWE

If it's a question of my social standing, my father was Sir George Crewe. You've heard of him, perhaps?

MISTRESS AMANDA MINCHIN

Oh, naturally.

CAPTAIN REGINALD CREWE

And the best financial references I could give you would be the directors of the South African holding syndicate. I'm the principal stockholder in the syndicate.

MISTRESS AMANDA MINCHIN

(indicating Bertie)

My brother, Captain Crewe: our professor of elocution and dramatics.

CAPTAIN REGINALD CREWE

(to Bertie)

How do you do?

HUBERT "BERTIE" MINCHIN

Charmed, I'm sure. I say, isn't the Eclipse diamond mines one of your holdings?

CAPTAIN REGINALD CREWE

One of the most important, of course.

HUBERT "BERTIE" MINCHIN

Of course, of course.

CAPTAIN REGINALD CREWE

I'm sorry to appear casual, Miss Minchin, but the situation is quite distressing. I sail in an hour from the East India Docks.

SARA CREWE

I expect you'll just have to take me to Africa with you, Daddy.

MISTRESS AMANDA MINCHIN

Oh, no. And what would a little girl like you do in Africa? Forgive me, Captain Crewe, I fear I've been overzealous—the reputation of my school, you know. One has to be so cautious. But after this interview, I can see at a glance, such a dear little child, it'll be a pleasure to have her with us.

SARA CREWE

Does that mean I've got to stay?

MISTRESS AMANDA MINCHIN

Yes, dear, you're to have that privilege, you and your little pony.

HUBERT "BERTIE" MINCHIN

What a dear little pony!

CAPTAIN REGINALD CREWE

This is made out to the school. Would it be enough for the moment?

MISTRESS AMANDA MINCHIN

Oh, quite.

HUBERT "BERTIE" MINCHIN

I should say it would. Why, it's stupendous.

CAPTAIN REGINALD CREWE

I beg your pardon, but haven't I seen you somewhere
before?

HUBERT "BERTIE" MINCHIN

It's quite possible, my dear captain.

CAPTAIN REGINALD CREWE

Your face is most familiar. Were you ever on the stage?
I seem to associate you with one of the old music halls.

MISTRESS AMANDA MINCHIN

Music halls! My brother on the stage! Ridiculous!

HUBERT "BERTIE" MINCHIN

Ridiculous indeed. You're quite right.

MISTRESS AMANDA MINCHIN

And now shall we look at little Sara's rooms?

**They go out into the hallway. Miss Rose is leading some girl
pupils down a set of stairs.**

MISTRESS AMANDA MINCHIN

Just a moment, Miss Rose. This is Miss Rose, one of my
most capable teachers. Captain Crewe has done us the
honor of placing his little daughter, Sara, with us.

CAPTAIN REGINALD CREWE

How'd you do, Miss Rose?

MISS ROSE

How do you do, Captain Crewe? We shall do everything we can to make your little girl happy.

CAPTAIN REGINALD CREWE

I'm sure you will.

MISTRESS AMANDA MINCHIN

Children, we have a new pupil, Sara Crewe. Say, how'd you do to her?

CHILDREN
(in unison)

How do you do?

Sara curtsies.

SARA CREWE

I'm very well, thank you.

Lavinia and Jessie, still on the stairs, look at each other and giggle.

MISTRESS AMANDA MINCHIN

Lavinia, Jesse, that will do. You may proceed, Miss Rose.

Miss Rose leads her class the rest of the way down the stairs.

MISS ROSE

Children.

SCHOOLGIRL 1

She's just like a little princess, isn't she?

SCHOOLGIRL 2

That's what she is—a princess. And I expect now, some people around here won't think they're so smart.

Lavinia and Jessie are right behind these girls. They look at each other superciliously.

LAVINIA

Oh, won't they? Wait and see. Princess indeed!

Captain Crewe, Miss Minchin, and Sara go up to the second floor.

MISTRESS AMANDA MINCHIN

Fortunately, the rooms have just been papered, and the fireplace has an excellent draft.

SARA CREWE

But I thought you didn't have any rooms.

MISTRESS AMANDA MINCHIN

But I didn't know then what a dear little girl was coming.

Miss Minchin goes in the room. The captain and Sara are still on the landing.

SARA CREWE

But why does that make more rooms, Daddy?

CAPTAIN REGINALD CREWE

Shush.

Captain Crewe and Sara follow Miss Minchin into the room.

MISTRESS AMANDA MINCHIN

Lady Bellis' little daughter's only recently vacated the rooms—our best suite, of course.

CAPTAIN REGINALD CREWE

Hmm. Do you think you could brighten it up a bit? I'd like it made as gay as possible. I brought a few things from India, but perhaps you could buy whatever else is necessary.

MISTRESS AMANDA MINCHIN

With pleasure, Captain Crewe.

CAPTAIN REGINALD CREWE

I'd like Sara to ride every afternoon, if the weather's all right.

MISTRESS AMANDA MINCHIN

Of course. Fortunately, we have a splendid riding master.

CAPTAIN REGINALD CREWE

I expect you to think I'm completely spoiling the child. And no doubt you're right. But actually it's good for her. She's much too inclined to bury her little nose in a book and keep it there until someone lures her out of it. You see, Miss Minchin, Sara has no mother, and we've never been separated for more than a few days.

MISTRESS AMANDA MINCHIN

How touching.

CAPTAIN REGINALD CREWE

This is going to be very hard for her.

MISTRESS AMANDA MINCHIN

Have no fear, Captain Crewe, I'm a mother to all my little girls. And now I leave you to your farewell.

SARA CREWE

How much longer have we got, Daddy?

CAPTAIN REGINALD CREWE

Only a few minutes, darling.

They go to a settee. Captain Crewe sits down, and Sara stands next to him. They embrace, and Sara strokes his cheek.

CAPTAIN REGINALD CREWE

You are learning me by heart, little Sara.

SARA CREWE

No, Daddy, I *know* you by heart. You are inside my heart.

CAPTAIN REGINALD CREWE

We are going to be brave, aren't we? I tell you what, let's pretend we're back in India, as I'm going away with a troop for a few days, shall we? We've fought this kind of battle before, haven't we? And you've never cried once when I went away. Remember?

SARA CREWE

Yes, Daddy.

CAPTAIN REGINALD CREWE

Well, this is going to be our hardest battle, but we'll be good soldiers, won't we?

SARA CREWE

Yes, Daddy.

They hug.

CAPTAIN REGINALD CREWE

Should we say goodbye like we used to at home?

SARA CREWE

Yes, Daddy.

CAPTAIN REGINALD CREWE

All right then. Chin up. Go to the window and look out.

Sara goes to the window and looks out, then turns around to her father.

CAPTAIN REGINALD CREWE

Now say it as we used to: My Daddy has to go away. But he'll return most any day. Any moment I may see my daddy coming back to me.

SARA CREWE

My Daddy has to go away, but he'll return most any day.

Sara, crying, turns and rushes into Captain Crewe's arms.

SARA CREWE

Any . . . I can't do it this time. I can't do it. You're crying too.

CAPTAIN REGINALD CREWE

Afraid we're not quite such good soldiers as we thought.

SARA CREWE

Oh yes, we are. I can do it now: My daddy has to go away. But he'll return most any day. Any moment, I may see my daddy coming back to me.

She turns away and sobs.

Now Sara is alone in her room, fastening the buttons on her boot with a buttonhook.

SARA CREWE

I'll do it. I will. I'll pretend this is part of a war. You'll be the enemy and you'll be my trusty lance. Now ready, aim, fire. Oh. Ouch. I guess we'll have to call on reserves.

She goes to the window and opens it. She sees Ram Dass in the window of the house opposite, in Indian dress, with a turban. Rani, a brightly colored parrot, is on a perch next to him.

SARA

(greets him in Hindustani)

RAM DASS

Good morning, Miss. Sahib speaks Hindustani.

SARA CREWE

I've lived in India all my life. [*Indian language*].

DAM DASS

[*Indian language*]. Missy Sahib is going to live in England now?

SARA CREWE

Only until my father gets through making the Boers behave.

DAM DASS

The sahib is then a soldier?

SARA CREWE

Yes. My father's a captain. Captain Crewe. I'm Sara. What is your name?

RAM DASS

I am Ram Dass, servant to the honorable Lord Wickham, and to her Ladyship Rani.

Lord Wickham comes into Ram Dass's room.

LORD WICKHAM

Ram Dass. Ram Dass.

RAM DASS

Yes, sir.

LORD WICKHAM

Why the duce are you dawdling here? Finish with that bird, and get on with your work.

SARA CREWE

Good morning.

LORD WICKHAM

How'd you do.

He goes off.

SARA CREWE TO RAM DASS

I'll be here at the window almost every morning in case you want to talk about India.

Miss Rose comes into Sara's room. Sara turns toward her.

ROSE

Morning, Sara.

SARA CREWE

Oh, good morning.

ROSE

Ready for breakfast, dear?

SARA CREWE

Well, I'm trying to be, but I don't seem to be very good
at these buttons. My thumb gets lost in the hole.

ROSE

Here, let me help you. Buttons are a bother, aren't they?

SARA CREWE

I never had to button anything before, but I'll learn.

ROSE

I'm sure you will. Here, put your shoe up.

There is a knock on the door.

ROSE

Come in. Good morning, Becky.

Becky comes in. She has an armful of girls' boots.

BECKY

Good morning. Has the young lady any boots to put
down?

SARA CREWE

Well, only the pair I wore yesterday. I'll get them.

**Sara runs to the bed and pulls out her boots from under the
bed.**

BECKY

I'll get them, Miss.

Becky follows her but falls down.

BECKY

Oh, I beg your pardon, Miss!

SARA CREWE

Are you hurt?

BECKY

No, Miss. You must not be helping me, Miss.

SARA CREWE

Hold out your arms. I'll pile them on.

Becky holds out her arms and Sara piles her boots on them.

BECKY

Oh, no, Miss. If Miss Minchin was to see. . .

SARA CREWE

You think you can hold two more?

BECKY

Yes. Miss.

SARA CREWE

There you are. Are you all right? You take care of all those?

BECKY

Yes, Miss.

ROSE

And she does them beautifully.

BECKY

Ah, thank you, Miss.

SARA CREWE

Thank you for doing my shoes.

Sara approaches Becky, who back into the open door, closing it.

BECKY

Oh. Oh, I'm sorry.

SARA CREWE

That's all right. Goodbye, Becky.

Sara opens the door.

BECKY

Goodbye.

SARA CREWE

Bye.

Becky goes out, and Sara closes the door behind her.

SARA CREWE

Well, perhaps this isn't going to be such a bad school after all, with you and Becky here.

ROSE

Oh, we'll have to hurry, dear. Miss Minchin doesn't like anyone to be late.

SARA CREWE

Tell me, Miss Rose, do you think Miss Minchin could
be as cross as she looks?

Rose smiles and shakes her head noncommittally.

SARA CREWE

What will I have to do today?

ROSE

Well, after breakfast, you'll have a class in arithmetic.

SARA CREWE

Arithmetic.

ROSE

Then English, then French, then one in elocution and
deportment, history, and geography.

SARA CREWE

Ew, I'm going to be a busy person, aren't I? When do I
get to ride my pony?

ROSE

Later this afternoon, about 4 o'clock.

SARA CREW

Oh!

**The scene is now in the dining room. The girls are assembled
standing at their places. Miss Minchin is standing at the head
of the table, along with Bertie, who is behind her.**

MISTRESS AMANDA MINCHIN

Children, our new pupil, Sara Crewe, will be down presently. As you've seen, Captain Crewe is a very delightful man, and their family is most distinguished. I should expect you to treat her accordingly. Now you may take your places.

Rose comes in with Sara.

ROSE

Good morning.

MISTRESS AMANDA MINCHIN

Ah, good morning, Sara.

SARA CREWE

Good morning.

MISTRESS AMANDA MINCHIN

I'm so happy you feel like joining us this morning. Did you sleep well?

SARA CREWE

No, I didn't, thank you.

MISTRESS AMANDA MINCHIN

Come, dear. Lavinia, you and Jessie will move down one place. Sara will be seated at my right after this.

LAVINIA

Why, Miss Minchin, this has always been my place.

MISTRESS AMANDA MINCHIN

Lavinia!

Lavinia ungraciously moves over one place as instructed. They all sit down, Sara on Miss Minchin's right. Two maids bring in food, and Miss Minchin raps on her glass.

MISTRESS AMANDA MINCHIN

For this food, and all the bountiful gifts bestowed upon us, we are duly grateful, and do now give thanks.

Mistress Minchin has two eggs in egg cups set in front of her. Sara puts some salt on her own plate.

MISTRESS AMANDA MINCHIN

Why are you putting salt on your plate, dear?

SARA CREWE

Just in case you should ask me to have one of your eggs.

General laughter. Bertie groans.

Now the scene is in the stable. Sandy, the groom, is grooming a black-and-white pony. Geoffrey Hamilton comes in.

SANDY

Mr. Geoffrey, Will I saddle the pony for the wee lassie?

GEOFFREY HAMILTON

I think not, Sandy. We best use the Mayor for her first few lessons.

SANDY

Very good, sir. Come on, lad.

Sandy leads the pony out. Miss Rose comes in with Sara.

GEOFFREY HAMILTON

Hello, there.

ROSE

Hello, Geoffrey.

Geoffrey takes Miss Rose affectionately by the hands.

GEOFFREY HAMILTON

What luck! The old girl allowed you to come out.

ROSE

Sara, this is Mr. Geoffrey Hamilton. Little Miss Crewe
is our new pupil.

SARA CREWE

How do you do?

GEOFFREY HAMILTON

How do you do? I believe I'm to teach you to ride.

SARA CREWE

Teach me?

GEOFFREY HAMILTON

And that means two bob extra for me.

SARA CREWE

Oh, is two bob a great deal of money?

GEOFFREY HAMILTON

Values are comparative. In my present state, it's a
fortune.

SARA CREWE

Well, in that case, I guess I'd better be taught. Is my
pony ready?

GEOFFREY HAMILTON

I think we'd best start you out on something a little tamer, huh?

SARA CREWE

Oh, then hadn't I better explain things to my pony? He might feel hurt.

GEOFFREY HAMILTON

Right you are. Ponies are very sensitive creatures. Explain the whole thing to him thoroughly. He's right there by the arch.

SARA CREWE

It may take me some time.

GEOFFREY HAMILTON

That's quite all right. We'll wait here in the tack room.

SARA CREWE

All right.

Sara goes into a stall, where her pony, General, is lying down.

SARA CREWE

Oh, General. You're glad to see me? Well, Mr. Geoffrey's going to give me something tamer than you. I'm afraid it isn't going to be much of a ride.

In the tack room:

GEOFFREY HAMILTON

Rose, something's wrong. What is it?

ROSE

Miss Minchin's taking away my Thursday afternoons.

But why?

ROSE

We must have been seen together.

GEOFFREY HAMILTON

Well, does that mean that I can never see you alone again?

ROSE

Of course not, darling. No matter what Miss. Minchin says, we'll find a way.

GEOFFREY HAMILTON

I can't understand the woman. What is she afraid of? Why shouldn't we see one another?

ROSE

Gossip, I suppose. She only lives for that school, and her ideas of propriety and snobbishness.

GEOFFREY HAMILTON

Fiddlesticks. She's afraid of losing an excellent teacher whom she gets for nothing. I won't stand for it. I'll have a talk with her myself.

ROSE

Oh, no, darling, you mustn't do that. She would only discharge us both.

GEOFFREY HAMILTON

She may not have the chance if things continue to pop in South Africa.

ROSE

You mean you might go?

GEOFFREY HAMILTON

Wouldn't you want me to, if they called for volunteers?

ROSE

Of course, darling, you'd have to. Oh, Geoffrey!

GEOFFREY HAMILTON

There's nothing to worry about now, dear. This poor rumpus will never get that serious.

They kiss. Sara comes in and sees them, then tactfully leaves before they notice her.
Sara goes back to General's stall and strokes the pony.

SARA CREWE

I expect I'll have to make my visits a little longer.

In the front hall, Bertie Minchin is sorting through a stack of mail. Becky is watching.

BECKY

Oh, Mr. Bertie, is there one this morning for the little princess?

HUBERT "BERTIE" MINCHIN

We shall see, my child, we shall see.

BECKY

If she doesn't hear from my father ever so often, her eyes get that sad. It hurts me to look on her.

HUBERT "BERTIE" MINCHIN

Have no fear, little one, there's a letter for her this time.

BECKY

Oh, am I glad, sir!

Becky goes off. A maid is dusting the railing on the stairs. Bertie tweaks her ear flirtatiously. She giggles. He goes upstairs.

Bertie arrives on the second-floor landing. He is in a spry mood and begins to dance and sing. Sara, seeing him, begins to sing and dance too.

Song: "The Old Kent Road"

As the song and dance end, Bertie playfully hands her the letter, and Sara blows him a kiss. She takes it and goes into her room, where she finds Miss Rose. Sara opens the letter and is reading it.

ROSE

A letter?

SARA CREWE

It's from my daddy.

ROSE

Oh, how nice.

SARA CREWE

But it isn't, it's very bad news.

ROSE

Really. What's the matter, dear?

SARA CREWE

He says the Boers are behaving not quite as he expected. He may not get here in time for my birthday,

ROSE

But that's months off. So many things may happen before then. He may still come, you know.

SARA CREWE
(reading)

"I'm writing Miss Minchin to give you a birthday party, such as I should give you if I were there. You are to go on a regular spree; buy anything and everything your heart desires. Now, last and most important of all, my darling, I want you to pause at exactly 2 o'clock on your birthday. Close your eyes and send me a kiss, for my eyes also will be closed, and I will be giving you a kiss too." Isn't he the most wonderful man in all the world?"

Miss Rose kisses Sara on the forehead.

ROSE

With one exception.

SARA CREWE

Well, Mr. Geoffrey is very nice.

They hear the sound of a marching band outside, and they go to the window. Outside they see columns of British troops marching by. Crowds are cheering.

SARA

What's that? Who are they, Miss Rose?

ROSE

They're the volunteers.

SARA CREWE

Are they going to South Africa too?

ROSE

Yes, dear. They're going to the relief some of our poor soldiers at Mafeking.

SARA CREWE

Something's the matter with our soldiers at Mafeking?

MISS ROSE

The Boers have them all cut off and we've been unable to break through their lines to get help to them. They're sick and hungry, dear, and desperate. They're holding out like true British soldiers.

Sara runs into her room and looks at the postmark on the letter. It says, "Mafeking. Besieged."

SARA CREWE

Miss Rose, my daddy's in Mafeking.

Sara bursts into tears.

ROSE

Oh darling, I'm so sorry. I didn't know.

SARA CREWE

Oh, Miss Rose.

Rose embraces her.

ROSE

Darling, you mustn't cry. I'm sure he'll be all right.

In the front hallway, Martha, a maid, opens the door for Geoffrey, who comes in. He is in riding habit.

MARTHA

Good afternoon, Mr. Geoffrey.

GEOFFREY HAMILTON

Good afternoon, Martha. Is Miss Sara ready for her ride?

MARTHA

Yes, sir. She should be down presently.

He sees Miss Rose and Sara going down the stairs. Sara is in a riding habit too.

GEOFFREY HAMILTON

Thanks. Oh, are we all ready?

ROSE

Hello, Geoffrey.

GEOFFREY HAMILTON

The two most beautiful ladies in the world!

(to Miss Rose)

Well, you're not in your riding things!

ROSE

Oh, I can't go today. Ermengarde needs extra tutoring.

GEOFFREY HAMILTON

Oh, will you take all afternoon?

ROSE

I'm afraid so. I have to stay with it until she can spell "Constantinople."

GEOFFREY HAMILTON

Good heaven, that may take months!

ROSE

You leave that to me.

He kisses her hand. Miss Rose goes upstairs.

GEOFFREY HAMILTON

(to Sara)

Shall we go? Have you been crying? But you have! There are still tears in your eyes.

SARA CREWE

It's just this London fog.

GEOFFREY HAMILTON

Oh, well, if that's all, let's be off, shall we?

Sara and Geoffrey go out onto the stoop.

SARA CREWE

Mr. Geoffrey, would you mind very much if we didn't ride today?

GEOFFREY HAMILTON

Not at all, dear. But may I ask why not?

SARA CREWE

I'd like to talk to you.

GEOFFREY HAMILTON

All right.

She sits down on a stair. Geoffrey sits down next to her.

SARA CREWE

It's about Mafeking. Are the soldiers really starving and sick and cut off from everything? You see, my father's there, and I've got to know.

GEOFFREY HAMILTON

Oh, it's not as bad as all that. Our men aren't having an easy time of it, it's true, but they're holding out and we are sending fresh troops every day, you know. Why, they'll be relieving Mafeking in no time at all now.

SARA CREWE

It's getting harder every day to pretend my father's safe.

GEOFFREY HAMILTON

Don't you worry. See, I'll let you in on a little secret. I enlisted today. And while I don't want Miss Rose to know quite yet, I'll be going over there shortly myself.

SARA CREWE

To Mafeking? Then perhaps you can help my father.

GEOFFREY HAMILTON

Right there. We'll get him out.

Lord Wickham approaches from the street with Ram Dass behind him.

LORD WICKHAM
(to Geoffrey)

What the blazes are you doing here?

GEOFFREY HAMILTON

Hello.

LORD WICKHAM

Answer me, you insolent puppy. What are you doing here?

GEOFFREY HAMILTON

Don't be frightened, Sara, it's only my grandfather.

LORD WICKHAM

Don't you believe him, young woman, I disowned him the day he was born.

GEOFFREY HAMILTON

And we're really very fond of each other.

LORD WICKHAM

Of course we are. What? We're nothing of the kind.

GEOFFREY HAMILTON

As a favor to me, will you please stop shouting at my best-paying pupil?

LORD WICKHAM

Pupil? Paying? what are you talking about?

GEOFFREY HAMILTON

I am master of the horse in this exclusive seminary for young ladies.

LORD WICKHAM

You take advantage of my absence to become a riding master, and next door to my own house! Where's your family pride, boy?

Sara goes over to Ram Dass. who covers her ears with his hands.

GEOFFREY HAMILTON

Well, sir, one must eat, and family pride is a pretty thin diet.

LORD WICKHAM

Oh, blackmail, eh? You think I'll buy you off?

GEOFFREY HAMILTON

I hadn't thought of that, but it's not a bad idea.

LORD WICKHAM

Well, I'll see you hanged, drawn, and quartered first. Wait until I see the woman who runs this school. I'll put a spoke in your wheel.

GEOFFREY HAMILTON

Do! She'd love to know my grandfather is Lord Wickham. She'll probably raise my salary.

RAM DASS

They have finished, Missy Sahib. Lord Wickham is coming.

SARA CREWE

Then I'm going.

LORD WICKHAM

Young pup, just like his father. Riding master. Blah!

Lord Wickham storms off.

SARA CREWE

Hey, you're fond of him, but I don't think he's very fond of you.

GEOFFREY HAMILTON

Oh, he's harmless. His bark's worse than his bite.

SARA CREWE

I should hope so. Why is he so mad at you?

GEOFFREY HAMILTON

Oh, he isn't really. He was angry with my father. I'm mixed up in their quarrel. What he really wants is to have me come begging to him for help. He'd be eating out of my hand if I would.

SARA CREWE

I don't think I'd care to have him eating out of *my* hand.

GEOFFREY HAMILTON

How would you like to have *me* eating out of your hand?

SARA CREWE

You, who? That would be different.

GEOFFREY HAMILTON

Well, I shall. Do me a favor. A very important one.

SARA CREWE

Oh, could I?

GEOFFREY HAMILTON

I've got an idea that you're the only one in the world who could. I want you to get Miss Rose to go shopping with you next Wednesday.

SARA CREWE

Shopping?

GEOFFREY HAMILTON

Well, shopping's as good an excuse as any for Miss Minchin. Honestly . . .

Geoffrey bends over and whispers something in Sara's ear.

SARA CREWE

Really? To Miss Rose? She said she would? Oh, that's wonderful. No, not a soul. Not even Emily.

GEOFFREY HAMILTON

Good girl. Now I've got to go. I have to do some preliminary shopping.

SARA CREWE

You don't have to tell me what for—something gold and shiny.

GEOFFREY HAMILTON

Right you are!
Sara, outside Miss Minchin's office, knocks on the door.

MISTRESS AMANDA MINCHIN

Come in.
                    (without looking up)
What do you want? I'm very busy.

SARA CREWE

Miss Minchin, I wanted to ask you something.

MISTRESS AMANDA MINCHIN

Oh, it's you! What do you want, dear?

SARA CREWE

I'm going to ask you a big favor.

MISTRESS AMANDA MINCHIN

Yes.

SARA CREWE

Mr. Geoffrey's leaving today for the war. He's been so very nice to me. I thought I ought to fill my social obligations by doing something for him. That's what you teach us, isn't it? When someone shows you a kindness, you show them one in return.

MISTRESS AMANDA MINCHIN

Well, doing something for Mr. Geoffrey scarcely comes under the rules of social obligations. But what is it you want to do for him?

SARA CREWE

May I have him for tea?

MISTRESS AMANDA MINCHIN

Here at the school?

SARA CREWE

Oh, couldn't I, please? Since he's going away to war.

MISTRESS AMANDA MINCHIN

Well, I suppose it would be permissible, since he was one of the teachers. You need not mention it to the other young ladies, however.

SARA CREWE

No, Miss Minchin. Thank you, Miss Minchin. Oh, thank you, Miss Minchin.

In the hallway in front of the drawing room, Sara marches back and forth in front of the door in a military manner. Inside the drawing room, Miss Rose and Geoffrey are sitting next to each other on the settee. Geoffrey is in military uniform.

ROSE

We must eat something after all the trouble little Sara's gone to.

GEOFFREY HAMILTON

I think she'll understand. You've forgotten your ring!

ROSE

No, I have it.

(She pulls the ring out from under her shirtwaist.)

See, I'm always afraid I'll forget and wear it in front of Miss Minchin. I did yesterday and fortunately for us, she didn't see it.

GEOFFREY HAMILTON

Oh, I'd love to tell the old girl.

ROSE

You can't do that yet, darling.

GEOFFREY HAMILTON

I know. You sorry you married me?

ROSE

As though you didn't know.

GEOFFREY HAMILTON

I only wanted you to tell me again. Oh my darling. I'll be living this last week over every moment that I'm away from you.

ROSE

And we'll be separated, won't we? Because I'll be living it over too.

Outside the room, Sara is still marching back and forth. Miss Minchin comes up to her.

MISTRESS AMANDA MINCHIN

I thought you were having Mr. Hamilton to tea?

SARA CREWE

I am. I mean, I was, but . . .

MISTRESS AMANDA MINCHIN

Who's in that room?

SARA CREWE

Oh, please don't go in there, Ms. Minchin.

GEOFFREY HAMILTON

Miss Minchin, Miss Rose and I . . .

ROSE

We were saying goodbye, Miss Minchin.

MISTRESS AMANDA MINCHIN

How dare you risk the reputation of my school in this manner?

GEOFFREY HAMILTON

Nothing's happened that damages your precious school's reputation. As a matter of fact, Miss Rose and I . . .

ROSE

Geoffrey, for my sake.

SARA CREWE

Oh, please Miss Minchin, it was all my fault.

MISTRESS AMANDA MINCHIN

Silence! Since you are here merely to say goodbye, please do so now.

Miss Rose and Geoffrey hold each other by the arms. They seem about to kiss but do not.

ROSE

Bye, Geoffrey.

SARA CREWE

Bye, Mr. Geoffrey.

GEOFFREY HAMILTON

Bye, dear.

MISTRESS AMANDA MINCHIN

Sara, I shall expect an explanation of this.

SARA CREWE

Yes, Ms. Minchin, as soon as I can think of one.

Miss Minchin looks aside, then goes out.
The scene changes. Outside on a wall is displayed the South Africa casualty list.

MALE SPEAKER 1

They've been cornered like rats for seven months.

MALE SPEAKER 2

I say send more troops to Mafeking, if it takes every man in England.

MALE SPEAKER 3

I am with you.

My, my boy! Oh, they killed my boy!

Back in Sara's room at night, she is saying her prayers kneeling before her bed.

SARA CREWE

I know soldiers are supposed to stand a lot, and my daddy is a good soldier. But they've waited so long for help. Please do something about Mafeking right away. Or they'll all be lost. My daddy won't come back.

Outside, Sara hears a marching band and a cheering crowd. She goes out on the balcony to see the crowd.

MALE SPEAKER

Mafeking is relieved! Mafeking is relieved!

SARA CREWE

Mafeking is relieved! Mafeking is relieved!

(to God)

Oh, Thank you for being so quick about it this time.

Sara rushes out into the hallway and starts knocking on everyone's door.

SARA CREWE

Get up, get up! Mafeking is relieved! Get up. Wake up, everybody! Mafeking is relieved!

Bertie comes downstairs.

SARA CREWE

Mr. Bertie, did you hear? Mafeking is relieved!

HUBERT "BERTIE" MINCHIN

Yes, darling, isn't it great news!

Miss Rose, Miss Minchin, and the other girls come out of their rooms. Sara hugs Miss Rose.

SARA CREWE

Oh, Miss Rose, they're saved! My daddy and Mr. Geoffrey are saved.

CHILDREN

What's wrong?

SARA CREWE

Nothing's wrong. Nothing. Nothing. Nothing. Mafeking is relieved!

MISTRESS AMANDA MINCHIN

Children!

SARA CREWE

Oh, Miss Minchin, isn't it wonderful! You hear them cheering?

CHILDREN

Yay, yay!

Everyone in the school is cheering and dancing around, singing "Auld Lang Syne." Then we hear "The British Grenadiers."

Sara is now among the crowd outside, waving a flag and jumping.

Now we see an elaborate birthday cake, with candles lit, and in the background, the girls of the school jumping up and down in the dining room. A wider shot of the dining room, decked out for Sara's party. Miss Minchin, Miss Rose, and Bertie are there as well. Miss Minchin calls the party to order.

MISTRESS AMANDA MINCHIN

Children, children. Attention, please. It is a happy circumstance that Sara's birthday should fall on a day when we're celebrating a glorious victory for Her Majesty's army. And now Sara, will you explain to the children your wishes about your birthday?

SARA CREWE

I'm very happy to have you here. And I thought I would like to give presents today. Not just receive them, because I wanted to show how grateful I am that my father has been rescued.

Children cheer.

MISTRESS AMANDA MINCHIN

Quiet, children, quiet.

SARA CREWE

Can we do the presents now?

They go to the gift table.

MISTRESS AMANDA MINCHIN

Yes, but your gift first, Sara. This is from me.

Miss Minchin presents Sara with a sewing kit.

SARA CREWE

Oh, thank you Miss Minchin, now all I need is to know how to sew!

MISTRESS AMANDA MINCHIN

And this from the entire school. Here are pictures of your native India.

SARA CREWE

Oh, thank you, ever and ever so much. I shan't have
to pretend nearly so hard when I want to make believe
I'm there.

MISTRESS AMANDA MINCHIN

And now do you want the others to have their presents?

SARA CREWE

Yes, I do, please. They're all over here. And your names
are all on them. Here you are, Miss Rose.

MISS ROSE

Oh, how nice.

SARA CREWE

And would you help with the other presents?

ROSE

Of course, dear.

SARA CREWE

And this is for you, Miss Minchin.

She hands a gift to Miss Minchin.

MISTRESS AMANDA MINCHIN

How thoughtful, Sara!

Becky looks in from the kitchen.

Sara goes off into the hallway, where Bertie is standing.
He presents her with a gift: a photo of himself in a music hall
outfit. The photo is in a silver frame.

HUBERT "BERTIE" MINCHIN

From one old trouper to another. Me in younger and happier days. When I was better known as Bubbling Bertie.

SARA CREWE

Oh, thank you. We'd better keep this present a secret.

HUBERT "BERTIE" MINCHIN

Mum's the word.

SARA CREWE

I should say it is. Here, this is from me.

She hands him a present. It is a Meerschaum pipe.

HUBERT "BERTIE" MINCHIN

Thank you.

SARA CREWE

I hope you like it.

HUBERT "BERTIE" MINCHIN

It's just what I wanted.

SARA CREWE

Mum's the word, you know.

HUBERT "BERTIE" MINCHIN

Rather.

Becky comes into the hallway.

BECKY

Oh, Miss, here is my present, Miss, and I aren't so very good.

It is a little cushion with pins stuck in it, spelling out the letters "MENNY APPY RETURNS."

SARA CREWE

Oh, thank you, Becky.

BECKY

They aren't nothing but pins, Miss, and the pins aren't so very new.

SARA CREW

Well, you dear Becky, you made it all yourself.

BECKY

Yes, Miss. I made it at nights. I knew you could pretend it was satin with diamond pins stuck in.

SARA CREWE

It's beautiful, Becky. I shall love it.

BECKY

Really, Miss, the material aren't very new.

SARA CREWE

And this isn't so very new either. It's my present to you.

BECKY

A present for me, Miss?

SARA CREWE

Yes, Becky, with my love.

BECKY

Oh, what is it, Miss?

It is a scarab with hieroglyphic writing, contained in a locket with a chain.

SARA CREWE

It's a scarab from Egypt. My daddy gave it to me because it brings good luck. I'd rather you have it than anyone else I know.

BECKY

Oh, no, Miss. I think I'm going to faint.

SARA CREWE

Oh, no Becky, not now. I have lots more presents for you too in my room.

BECKY

I don't know what to say, Miss.

SARA CREWE

You are sweet, Becky.

Back in the dining room, two of the girls are showing their gifts to Miss Minchin.

MISTRESS AMANDA MINCHIN

Yes, it's very nice.

SCHOOL GIRL

Oh, look at mine, Miss Minchin!

Mrs. O'Connell, the housekeeper, comes in.

MRS. O'CONNELL

Beg pardon, Miss.

MISTRESS AMANDA MINCHIN

Yes.

MRS. O'CONNELL

Mr. Barrows of Barrows Skipper is here to see you.

MISTRESS AMANDA MINCHIN

Today? I didn't send for him.

MRS. O'CONNELL

He seems very much upset about something. He's waiting in your office.

MISTRESS AMANDA MINCHIN

Very well. I'll go at once.

She goes out. Miss Rose is examining the scarf that is Sara's gift to her.

SARA CREWE

Miss Rose!

ROSE

The scarf is beautiful!

SARA CREWE

Miss Rose, will you be sure to tell me when it's almost 2 o'clock?

ROSE

Of course, dear.

SARA CREWE

You know I have a very special appointment with my daddy. He has to be thinking of me at exactly 2 o'clock.

ROSE

I'll watch the time.

SARA CREWE

Thank you, Miss Rose.

SCHOOLGIRL

Sara, thank you for the handkerchiefs, they're lovely. Don't you think it's time to cut the cake?

SARA CREWE

Oh yes, the cake.

Mr. Barrows, a solicitor, is standing in Miss Minchin's office. She comes in.

MISTRESS AMANDA MINCHIN

Please be seated, Mr. Barrows.

MR. BARROWS

How much did you advance for this birthday? Quite a sum, I suspect.

MISTRESS AMANDA MINCHIN

What does it matter? Captain Crewe is a very wealthy man. His check will be here shortly.

MR. BARROWS

No Miss Minchin, there'll be no check.

MISTRESS AMANDA MINCHIN

What? What do you mean by that?

MR. BARROWS

The late Captain Crewe . . .

MISTRESS AMANDA MINCHIN

The late Captain Crewe!

MR. BARROWS

Captain Crewe is dead. He was so reported in the list this morning. Moreover, he died a bankrupt.

MISTRESS AMANDA MINCHIN

Bankrupt. But his property, his mines?

MR. BARROWS

His property and his mines were confiscated by the enemy.

MISTRESS AMANDA MINCHIN

You mean to tell me that that child is penniless? That she's left on my hands with nothing?

MR. BARROWS

She's certainly left penniless, and she's certainly left on your hands. She hasn't a relative in the world that we know of.

MISTRESS AMANDA MINCHIN

But her father's account is overdrawn. I was expecting a check in advance, the money for this party.

MR. BARROWS

So I understand.

MISTRESS AMANDA MINCHIN

But this is monstrous.

Back in the dining room, Sara is standing in front of her lit cake.

ROSE

Now you have to make a wish and blow out all the candles with one breath.

SARA CREWE

My wish is that my father will come back very soon.

ROSE

Now take a big breath.

Sara blows out all the candles but one.

SARA CREWE

I haven't got very good lungs, have I?

Back in Miss Minchin's office:

MISTRESS AMANDA MINCHIN

I'll turn her out in the streets!

MR. BARROWS

You think that's wise, Miss Minchin? The reputation of your school, you know?

MISTRESS AMANDA MINCHIN

My school?

MR. BARROWS

Well, the report might get about and it might not sound well to the parents of some of your other pupils.

MISTRESS AMANDA MINCHIN

Yes, that is so.

MR. BARROWS

Of course the child could be made to serve in your employ until her indebtedness is worked out.

MISTRESS AMANDA MINCHIN

But that would take years.

MR. BARROWS

Quite so. But at least it's better than nothing.

Back in the dining room, the children are about to sit down for their cake.

ROSE

Hurry, children, your ice cream's melting.

SCHOOL GIRL

Thank you, Sara.

ROSE

Sara, it's almost 2 o'clock, darling.

SARA CREWE

Thank you, Miss Rose.

Sara goes into the pantry, holding her father's letter. The clock strikes two.

SARA CREWE

Oh, Daddy, I am thinking of you, and I know that wherever you are, you are thinking of me too.

Miss Rose comes in.

SARA CREWE

Oh, Miss Rose. I feel him with me, I really did.

ROSE

Miss Minchin wants you, dear.

SARA CREWE

Oh, all right.

Back in the dining room:

MISTRESS AMANDA MINCHIN

Children, you will leave your gifts here.

SARA CREWE

Why? Where are they going? Why can't they take the presents with them?

MISTRESS AMANDA MINCHIN

Because they're not yours to give.

SARA CREWE

But I don't understand.

MISTRESS AMANDA MINCHIN

You will later. Go to your room now.

SARA CREW

Miss Minchin?

MISTRESS AMANDA MINCHIN

Sara, go to your room . . . all of you.

The girls leave the dining room, leaving Miss Minchin, Miss Rose, and Bertie.

HUBERT "BERTIE" MINCHIN

Now will you tell me what it's all about?

ROSE

What has happened, Miss Minchin?

HUBERT "BERTIE" MINCHIN

Whatever did happen, you might have let her off a bit easier.

MISTRESS AMANDA MINCHIN

Silence! Captain Crewe is dead. His name appeared on the list today. He's left the child a pauper.

ROSE

Oh, Miss Minchin!

MISTRESS AMANDA MINCHIN

You had better tell her.

ROSE

Oh, I couldn't do that.

MISTRESS AMANDA MINCHIN

You will do as you are told.

Sara is in her room, pacing nervously. Miss Rose comes in.

SARA CREWE

Miss Rose, what's wrong? Why did Miss Minchin stop the party?

ROSE

Sara, I want to talk to you in a minute, dear. Oh, darling!

Miss Rose sits down in a chair and hugs Sara to her.

SARA CREWE

Oh, Miss Rose, what is it?

ROSE

Sara, you are a soldier's daughter, and you know that that means being brave and courageous, don't you, no matter what happens?

SARA CREWE

Oh, Miss Rose, is it something awful?

ROSE

Your father . . .

SARA CREWE

But my father's all right. Mafeking is relieved. You heard them say so.

ROSE

Help didn't get there soon enough, dear, for him. His name appeared on the list this morning.

SARA CREWE

You mean with the wounded?

ROSE

No, dear.

SARA CREWE

My daddy is . . .

ROSE

Sara, I'm so sorry.

SARA CREWE

It can't be. It isn't true. I won't believe it. He isn't dead, he isn't!

Miss Minchin comes into Sara's room.

MISTRESS AMANDA MINCHIN

(to Miss Rose)

Have you . . .

ROSE

Yes.

MISTRESS AMANDA MINCHIN

(to Rose)

You may go.

(to Sara)

Sara, you understand of course that these rooms can no longer be yours. Come with me.

They go out. Sara sadly takes her doll with her. They go into the hallway and up the stairs. Miss Minchin leads Sara into a dingy attic room.

MISS MINCHIN

This is to be your room in the future. I shall have to sell your furnishings and your clothes to pay part of the debt your father owed. Ordinarily, you would go to a charitable institution, but I'm going to let you remain here. There will be duties for you to perform, of course. I hope you appreciate my kindness in not sending you away.

Sara looks up at Miss Minchin, scowling. Miss Minchin, holding a black dress, hands it to Sara.

MISS MINCHIN

I was unable to find a black dress among your things. So one of the girls has given you this. You'd better take off that party frock and put this on. I'll send up some shoes.

• **55** •

Miss Minchin goes out. Sara is alone. Holding her doll, she says:

SARA CREWE

I don't believe it. I don't, I don't. My daddy has to go away, but he'll return most any day. Any moment I may see my daddy coming back to me.

In the dining room, the girls stand at the table waiting to be seated for breakfast.

SCHOOL GIRL 1

And Miss Minchin's going to sell all her things.

SCHOOL GIRL 2

It was beastly having to give back our presents.

LAVINIA

How do you feel now about your little princess?

Sara goes downstairs, where Becky is polishing the railing.

BECKY

Oh, Miss, is there anything I can do?

SARA CREWE

No. Becky. Thank you.

Sara is now in the dining room.

SCHOOLGIRL

Sara, I'm sorry.

Miss Minchin shoves the schoolgirl aside.

MISTRESS AMANDA MINCHIN

Sara, from now on you're not to sit with us. Return to your room and smooth down those curls, then go to the kitchen. Run along now. Girls! Lavinia, you may take your old place beside me.

Lavinia proudly takes her old seat back.

In the kitchen, Mrs. O'Connor, a maid, and Becky are at work.

SARA CREWE

Mrs. O'Connor.

MRS. O'CONNELL

Oh. So the mistress has sent you down to me, has she?

SARA CREWE

Miss Minchin said I'm to have my breakfast here.

MRS. O'CONNELL

You'll do more than eat your breakfast if you work for that one.

Mrs. O'Connell is stirring a pot of porridge.

SARA CREWE

I shall be glad to help.

MRS. O'CONNELL

You will, eh?

Becky, at the stove, is burning the toast.

Mrs. O'Connell rushes over to her.

MRS. O'CONNELL

Look at you, look what you're doing! For that you'll get no breakfast. Min, you better make some more toast for the misses.

MINNIE

That job coming up.

Mrs. O'Connell hands Sara a bowl of porridge.

MRS. O'CONNELL

Here's your breakfast. Take it over there. We don't associate with royalty.

BECKY

Let me wait on you, Miss.

MRS. O'CONNELL

(to Becky)

No, you don't. She can wait on herself. You can sit there and watch her eat. Perhaps that'll teach you a lesson.

SARA CREWE

Please, Mrs. O'Connell, may I give my breakfast to Becky? I'm not hungry this morning.

MRS. O'CONNELL

Give it to the cat if you like, and get to work. Wash them dishes.

Sara pushes her bowl of porridge to Becky.

BECKY

No, Miss. Oh, I don't want it.

In the hallway, Miss Rose passes Bertie.

HUBER "BERTIE" MINCHIN

The mail just came.

Rose goes and gets the mail. Miss Minchin accosts her.

MRS. AMANDA MINCHIN

Miss Rose, I'll take the mail, if you please.

Miss Rose goes off, looking back uneasily as she goes up the stairs.

Now Miss Minchin is in Lord Wickham's drawing room. She is holding Geoffrey's letter to Miss Rose. She reads it to Lord Wickham.

MISS MINCHIN

(reading)

"My darling girl, I have been half mad trying to find a way out for you since your letter reached me. But it has come. My grandfather has relented. I pray heaven that this money and my love will help you bear what lies ahead. Geoffrey."

LORD WICKHAM

You say this girl's a teacher at your school?

MRS. AMANDA MINCHIN

She was, until I discharged her today. We are not likely to hear from her again.

LORD WICKHAM

And I was prepared to turn over a handsome sum to that boy when he got back. Even made an ass of myself and sent him a check.

MRS. AMANDA MINCHIN

Then I was right to withhold this.

(She holds out a check.)

He made it over to her.

LORD WICKHAM

You're not very fond of the girl, are you?

MRS. AMANDA MINCHIN

Hardly, under the circumstances.

LORD WICKHAM

You're sure the girl has no legitimate claims on him?

MRS. AMANDA MINCHIN

I brought her up from a foundling. Is it likely she would not have consulted me if their love had been respectable?

LORD WICKHAM

Ram Dass!

Ram Dass comes in and bows.

RAM DASS

Yes, sir.

LORD WICKHAM

In future, if any letters or cables come from Mr. Geoffrey, they're to be returned, unopened.

RAM DASS

As you wish, sir.

In Sara's new, dismal room, Sara holds her doll closely. There is thunder and lightning outside. There is a knock on the door.

SARA CREWE

Becky! Come in, Becky.

Becky comes in.

BECKY

I am glad you aren't asleep, Miss. It's one of them lonely nights.

SARA CREWE

Yes. I wonder where Miss Rose is. I shall miss her terribly.

BECKY

We're all alone in the world now, aren't we, Miss?

SARA CREWE

No, no, we're not alone. There's my father, you know.

BECKY

Your father. But cook says he . . .

SARA CREWE

You mustn't say that. It isn't true. He's not dead. He's sick or wounded somewhere, he'd send for me, but he's not dead.

BECKY

How do you know, Miss?

SARA CREWE

Something inside tells me so. And sometimes I hear him calling for me.

BECKY

Oh no, Miss.

Miss Minchin, on the landing, hears Bertie in his room. She goes in. He is dressed in military uniform and smoking the Meerschaum pipe that Sara gave him.

HUBERT "BERTIE" MINCHIN
(Singing)

Oh, don't rob the children of the . . .

MRS. AMANDA MINCHIN
You're smoking!

HUBERT "BERTIE" MINCHIN
As you see. Today, my good woman, the British army is behind me.

MRS. AMANDA MINCHIN
That uniform! You are not going to war!

HUBERT "BERTIE" MINCHIN
Quite! To the very cannon's mouth if need be.

MRS. AMANDA MINCHIN
But why?

HUBERT "BERTIE" MINCHIN
Because, old girl, I'm fed to the teeth with your bullying, and your treatment of Rose and little Sara is the last straw. I prefer the less painful horrors of the battlefield.

MRS. AMANDA MINCHIN
Are you daring to criticize me?

HUBERT "BERTIE" MINCHIN

Astonishing, isn't it? But it proves that I'm competent to lead my men into the very jaws of death.

MRS. AMANDA MINCHIN

After this, you may never expect help from me again.

HUBERT "BERTIE" MINCHIN

I am quite calm, for if the bloodthirsty Boer spares me, the footlights will see Bubbling Bertie once again.

MRS. AMANDA MINCHIN

Hubert, you wouldn't do that to me?

HUBERT "BERTIE" MINCHIN

Oh, wouldn't I? Well, ta-ta, old girl!

Bertie picks up his bag and his umbrella. As he goes out, he raps Miss Minchin on the rear with the umbrella.

MRS. AMANDA MINCHIN

Oh!

Sara is in her new room. There is snow outside. She pours some water from a pitcher into a bowl and washes her face with it. Then she puts on a black coat and goes out.

We now see her walking in the snowy street. She accosts a man in military uniform who is limping and walking with a cane.

SARA CREWE

Could you please, sir?

MALE SPEAKER

Yes, lassie.

SARA CREWE

Were you at the siege of Mafeking?

MALE SPEAKER

Aye, that's where I stopped the bullet that stopped me.

SARA CREWE

Then did you know my father?

MALE SPEAKER

Your father? What might his name be, lassie?

SARA CREWE

Captain Reginald Crewe.

MALE SPEAKER

Your father a captain?

SARA CREW

Yes. They say he is dead, but I know it can't be. I've asked so many soldiers about him. I hope you can tell me.

MALE SPEAKER

No, lassie, I'm sorry. I can't. Why don't you ask in the hospital there? Maybe they'll have some record of him?

SARA CREWE

Thank you, sir. I will. If you please, sir.

Sara goes to the stoop of the hospital and sees Bertie in uniform. He is now wearing a moustache. She goes up to him, and they stand in the doorway.

HUBERT "BERTIE" MINCHIN

Why, the little princess, as I live!

SARA CREWE

It's Mr. Bertie!

HUBERT "BERTIE" MINCHIN

In person.

SARA CREWE

I thought you'd gone to war?

HUBERT "BERTIE" MINCHIN

No. Lord Roberts wanted me to, of course. But he said Bertie, old boy, the wounded need you. So you stay here and cheer up the brave lads who have fallen in our just cause. So I am practically in command of this hospital.

SARA CREWE

Oh, Mr. Bertie, can my father be in there?

HUBERT "BERTIE" MINCHIN

Your father, princess?

SARA CREWE

Yes. You see, I know he isn't dead, and I've been looking and looking. He could be among the wounded, couldn't he?

HUBERT "BERTIE" MINCHIN

Yes.

SARA CREWE

I'm almost sure he is, somewhere. If you're in charge, could I please look for me there?

HUBERT "BERTIE" MINCHIN

Well . . .

SARA CREW

Please.

HUBERT "BERTIE" MINCHIN

Yes, yes, of course you may. Things like that can happen, you know.

Inside the hospital, Sara and Bertie walk up a flight of stairs.

SARA CREWE

Mr. Bertie, why don't they salute you if you're in command here?

HUBERT "BERTIE" MINCHIN

Discipline in a hospital is rather relaxed.

SARA CREWE

Oh.

An orderly approaches Bertie on the stairs.

ORDERLY

Now, I say, Major, they're waiting for you in ward B. There's a lot of trash up there.

HUBERT "BERTIE" MINCHIN

Very good. I'll get one of my men to attend to it.

MALE SOLDIER

Get one of your what?

HUBERT "BERTIE" MINCHIN

Well, well, two of my men, then. Carry on.

Bertie and Sara are now on the landing of the second floor. A sergeant sees them as they walk past.

SERGEANT

Soldier!

HUBERT "BERTIE" MINCHIN

Sir.

MALE SOLDIER

What's this child doing before visiting hours?

HUBERT "BERTIE" MINCHIN

But, you see, sir . . .

SERGEANT

Well, well . . .

SARA CREWE

If you please sir, the major's helping me to find my father, sir.

SERGEANT

The major?

HUBERT "BERTIE" MINCHIN

To her, sir. You see we're old friends, sir. I knew her father, Captain Crewe, who is reported killed at Mafeking. The child is sure there's some mistake, so I'm helping her search among the wounded.

SARA CREWE

Could you tell me anything about my father, sir?

SERGEANT

Sorry, my dear, I can't.

The sergeant salutes Bertie ironically, winking.

SERGEANT

Carry on, Major.

HUBERT "BERTIE" MINCHIN

Yes, sir. Thank you, sir.

Bertie and Sara go into a hospital ward. Bertie approaches the nurse. Sara goes off, looking.

BERTIE

(whispering to the nurse)

This little girl's father's been killed, but she insists he's alive. Let her look around. We will try another ward.

Sara looks around and does not see her father.

They got into another ward, where wounded men in better shape are sitting around, playing cards.

WOUNDED SOLDIER

There's old Bertie. Give us a song, lad.

HUBERT "BERTIE" MINCHIN

Attention, man. Official inspection.

SARA CREWE

He isn't here either, but someone might know about him?

Sara goes up to a wounded soldier in a wheelchair.

SARA CREWE

If you please, sir, were you at the siege of Mafeking?

WOUNDED SOLDIER

I was there, darling. It's where I picked up the bug. It was no bigger than the seed of a thistledown that laid me low. Ah, the bugs down there are worse than their bullets.

SARA CREWE

And perhaps you didn't know my father.

WOUNDED SOLDIER

I definitely wouldn't have known me own father, with the fever that was on me.

SARA CREWE

Thank you, sir.

WOUNDED SOLDIER

It's all right, darling.

Sara goes up to another soldier, a younger man, blond, with a moustache, and deranged. He is cutting out a paper doll of a soldier.

DERANGED SOLDIER

Hello.

SARA CREWE

If you please, sir, were you with the troops at Mafeking?

DERANGED SOLDIER

Yes. Yes, of course I was. That's where I ran away, you know.

SARA CREWE

Then did you know my father, Captain Crewe?

DERANGED SOLDIER

Yes. Yes, of course.

(He holds up the paper doll.)

That's a fine-looking officer, isn't he? He ought to do well.

SARA CREWE

Where did you see my father last? Where is he now?

DERANGED SOLDIER

Where's who?

SARA CREWE

My father.

DERANGED SOLDIER

Well, one soldier more or less doesn't make any difference, you know? I'm making thousands and thousands for England. See, fine, strong fellas who won't be afraid as I was. I was afraid of the noise. That's why I ran away, you know.

Bertie comes up to them.

SARA CREWE

He said he knows my father, but he won't tell.

HUBERT "BERTIE" MINCHIN

He's living in a dream, Sara, he doesn't know what he's saying. Come along, dear.

WOUNDED SOLDIER 1

Don't go out of here; give us a song.

WOUNDED SOLDIER 2

Yes, a song, Bertie.

HUBERT "BERTIE" MINCHIN

How about it, dear? Shall we sing them a song to cheer them up? Our old specialty one?

SARA CREWE

Not today, Mr. Bertie.

HUBERT "BERTIE" MINCHIN

Oh, come on, darling, let's try and forget our own troubles and do something for these lads, shall we?

SARA CREWE

All right, I'll try.

HUBERT "BERTIE" MINCHIN

Oh you, darling. What about "The Old Kent Road"?

WOUNDED SOLDIER

That's the one. Mac here will play for you.

Mac strikes up his accordion.

WOUNDED SOLDIER

Have a go at it, Mac.

HUBERT "BERTIE" MINCHIN
(Sings "The Old Kent Road")

Bertie and Sara do a tap dance.

Now we see Bertie and Sara outside the front entrance of the hospital.

SARA CREWE

Mr. Bertie, would it be all right if I come again tomorrow?

HUBERT "BERTIE" MINCHIN

Shouldn't run away too often, princess. You might get punished, you know? I'll keep a sharp lookout whenever the wounded come in.

SARA CREWE

You don't really believe he'll ever come, do you?

HUBERT "BERTIE" MINCHIN

Yes, yes, of course I do. I've told you missing men often turn up.

SARA CREWE

Then I'd better come. You might not know him if he were very much changed.

HUBERT "BERTIE" MINCHIN

All right, dear, you come.

SARA CREWE

Goodbye, Mr. Bertie.

HUBERT "BERTIE" MINCHIN

Goodbye, dear.

At the open window of her room, Sara is throwing scraps of food to sparrows on the ledge outside.

SARA CREWE

Are you hungry? Here. Poor little things, there won't be any worms for you this morning.

The windows of the house next door open, and Ram Dass looks out. Rani the parrot is on his shoulder.

RAM DASS

Good morning, little Missy Sahib.

SARA CREWE

Good morning, Ram Dass.

RAM DASS

Feeding your little friends?

SARA CREWE

Yes, but I couldn't feed them very much after my supper last night.

RAM DASS

Oh, it is difficult for them when the snow comes.

Rani flies off of Ram Dass's shoulder and into Sara's room. Ram Dass leaps over to follow him.

RAM DASS

Rani, Rani!

Ronnie perches on an empty shelf.

SARA CREWE

Oh, Rani, Rani! You look as though you know you are being naughty and enjoying it.

RAM DASS

Rani, for shame!

SARA CREWE

Here she is, on the bookshelves.

RAM DASS

Bookshelves?

SARA CREWE

Oh, I forgot. I pretend they're bookshelves and filled with beautiful books.

RAM DASS

Then I'd better remove her before she ruins a set of Dickens, right? This is your room, Missy Sahib?

SARA CREWE

Yes. It's so little and so high above everything

(Ronnie squawks)

that it's almost like a nest in a tree. I can lie on my soft sofa and look up in the sky through that little window in the roof.

Ram Dass looks down at her bed.

RAM DASS

Sofa?

SARA CREWE

It looks more like a soft sofa when it's made up. And you imagine it has down quilts and lovely cushions to curl up on.

RAM DASS

There is a fire sometimes, of course.

SARA CREWE

Well, that is the hardest of all to imagine, especially at night. But it's lovely when you can. The grate is polished, and there's a nice bright coal scuttle on the hearth.

Becky rushes into the room.

BECKY

Oh, hurry, Miss, the cook wants you, and she's in an awful stew.

SARA

Oh, my goodness! Excuse me if I run. I have to go to the butcher's. I'll get my ears boxed if I don't hurry.

RAM DASS

Yes, Missy Sahib.

Sara and Becky run out. Ram Dass looks around, sad and perplexed, at the dismal little room.

In the kitchen, Mrs. O'Connell is kneading some bread. Minnie, the maid, is reading the newspaper. Sara is peeling potatoes in a bowl. Becky is at work as well.

MINNIE
(reading)

Listen to this: "Hospital ship *Mercy* arrives. 1200 wounded disembarked."

MRS. O'CONNELL

Does it give any of the names?

MINNIE

There ain't no list. Oh, I hope my poor Harry is among them.

MRS. O'CONNELL

A wounded husband is better than no husband at all, eh, Min?

SARA CREWE

(whispering to Becky)

Becky, I've got to get to the hospital before 9 o'clock when they close to visitors. Somehow I've got to.

BECKY

Yes, Miss.

Sara drops the bowl of potatoes, breaking it.

MRS. O'CONNELL

You clumsy ox! For that you'll whistle for your supper.

BECKY

Oh, ma'am, she didn't get no lunch. You put things away before she got back from the grocer's.

MRS. O'CONNELL

Who do you think you are talking to? You'll both go hungry. Now clean up this mess. Go on, get on with it.

Sara picks up the broken pieces of the bowl.

At the hospital, a doctor and his aide are walking to a ward.

AIDE

Some sorry cases in this batch, doctor.

DOCTOR 1

Yes, poor devils.

The doctor and aide go into the ward. A nurse and another doctor are standing by the bed of a patient. It is the delirious Captain Crewe with a bandage on his head.

DOCTOR 2

Hello, doctor.

NURSE

Doctor, this man is an unknown. His papers were lost. Delirium following malarial fever.

DOCTOR 2

We're very much concerned about him, sir.

DOCTOR 1

(reading the chart)

Anemia, heart action weak, respiration low. Well, that's to be expected.

DOCTOR 2

But his mind doesn't clear, sir. He has no lucid moments.

DOCTOR 1

Temporary paralysis of some nerve center or a blood clot, possibly.

DOCTOR 2

More likely to be the latter, sir. He received a nasty head wound.

CAPTAIN REGINALD CREWE

(deliriously)

Sara. Sara.

DOCTOR

He repeatedly called for this person Sara.

DOCTOR

You can't learn who this Sara is?

DOCTOR

No way of finding out, sir, until his identity is established.

CAPTAIN REGINALD CREWE

Sara, Sara.

Back in the kitchen, Sara and Becky are cleaning up. The
clock shows 8:10.

BECKY

You better go now, Miss. I'll finish up for you.

SARA CREWE

Thank you, Becky. I'll have to fly.

BECKY

Yes, Miss.

Mrs. Connell comes into the kitchen.

MRS. O'CONNELL

Here, hold your horses. Where do you think you are
going? Miss Lavinia wants some coal for the fire. Off
to it.

In the hallway, Sara is running with the coal scuttle. A little
schoolgirl approaches her.

SCHOOL GIRL

Oh, Sara, you look so tired, and you look hungry too.
Are you actually hungry, Sara?

SARA CREWE

Yes. I am hungry. I'm so hungry I could eat you!

Sara brings the scuttle full of coal into Lavinia's room. Lavinia
is on a chaise longue, reading.

LAVINIA

Put it on plenty. My father pays for it.

Sara empties the scuttle into the hearth and starts to rush off.

LAVINIA

Just a moment! Our princess seems to be in a hurry.
Could it be that she's going to a ball?

Sara is about to rush off, but Lavinia stops her.

LAVINIA

Come back here and clean up that hearth.

Sara goes back to the hearth, scrapes a couple of shovelfuls of
ash into it, then makes to leave.

LAVINIA

I'd like my shawl, the pink one. It's on my bed.

Sara throws the shawl at her.

LAVINIA

Cover me, please. I find the room a bit chilly.

Sara puts the cover hastily over Lavinia and rushes off.
    Sara runs through the streets of London as the 9 p.m. bell
tolls. She goes to the hospital and knocks on the door.

ATTENDANT 1
(inside)

Good night, chief.

ATTENDANT 2
(inside)

Good night.

Attendant 2 opens the door to Sara's knock.

ATTENDANT 2

Hello, princess. What are you doing out so late?

SARA CREWE

I've come to see the new soldiers who got here today.

ATTENDANT 2

Not tonight, my girl, it's closing time.

SARA CREWE

But I've got to. I ran away especially.

ATTENDANT 2

Nah, then, young 'un, take it easy.

SARA CREWE

Please let me in. I'm sure he is here this time.

ATTENDANT 2

You're sure every time, princess, I'm sorry. You run on home and come back tomorrow morning. That's a good little girl. All right. Good night, ma'am.

Sara walks off sadly into the night.

In the hospital ward, three doctors, an aide, and a nurse are standing besides Captain Crewe's bed.

DOCTOR 1

He will recover from the effects of the fever. But I'm convinced there is brain pressure.

DOCTOR 2

You advise an operation then?

DOCTOR 1

Yes. Do you agree?

DOCTOR 3

I do. Dr. McNeish in Edinburgh is the man.

DOCTOR

Yes, splendid, splendid.

DOCTOR

List this man for removal to Edinburgh in the morning.

NURSE

Yes, Doctor.

CAPTAIN REGINALD CREWE

Sara.

Miss Minchin sees Sara come in. She follows her up to her room.

MISTRESS AMANDA MINCHIN

Sara, where have you been? Answer me. You've been out, haven't you?

SARA CREWE

Yes. Miss Manchin.

MISTRESS AMANDA MINCHIN

What do you mean by disobeying my orders?

SARA CREWE

I had to. I had to look for my father.

MISTRESS AMANDA MINCHIN

This ridiculous search for your father! All this making believe and refusing to face facts. It's indecent. I've
had enough of it. You must realize once and for all
that your father is dead.

SARA CREWE

Don't you say that. He's not dead. He's not. And you
can't stop me from looking for him either.

MISTRESS AMANDA MINCHIN

How dare you speak to me in that manner! You evil
little . . . ! I'll attend you further in the morning.

Miss Minchin storms out. Sara addresses her doll.

SARA CREWE

I can't be a good soldier much longer. I'm cold, and I'm
hungry too. Do you hear? No. You don't hear. You don't
hear. And you don't care. You're nothing but a doll. A
doll! You never had a heart to make you feel. You're
just a doll.

She pushes her doll off the chair, sobbing.

Ram Dass looks out the window next door at her.

Sara, in bed, has a dream. In it, she is a princess with a
crown, seated on a throne. A page presents her a scepter on a
pillow. Two lavishly dressed ladies preen her. Two others lay
an ermine stole at her feet. A jester (Bertie) comes in, dances
around, and sits down at the side of Sara's throne.

A trumpet fanfare announces a troupe of three harp play-
ers that enter, led by a drum major, followed by a line of chefs
holding huge platters of food, followed by musicians and three
pages holding an enormous birthday pie, out of which birds
fly out as they place it before Princess Sara. Another trumpet
fanfare announces a vizier, who enters. (It is Ram Dass.)

VIZIER

Your Highness, please forgive me, but something has gone amiss. There is an angry woman outside to report a stolen kiss.

PRINCESS

Tell her she must go away, come around some other day.

VIZIER

I have told her, but she won't. You must see her; if you don't, she'll scream her head off.

JESTER

Tell her to hush.

MALE SPEAKER

She won't be hushed.

MALE SPEAKER

Then tell her to shush.

MALE SPEAKER

I am afraid she won't be shushed.

A witchlike figure (Miss Mintin) in a black gown with a hat of two horns comes in.

WITCH

I won't be shushed. I won't be hushed. I know my rights. I know the law and I know also what I saw.

PRINCESS

What did you see?

I saw him.

PRINCESS

You saw who? I mean whom?

WITCH

I saw that lad steal a kiss from that shameless little miss.

Geoffrey and Miss Rose are brought in, dressed like a shepherd and a medieval maiden.

WITCH

Don't be fooled by all their shyness. They're a wicked pair, your highness. There's a law, I understand, against kissing in this land.

VIZIER

There is a law that reads like this: "No one is to steal a kiss."

JESTER

Ah, but Princess, I have a feeling this is not a case of stealing.

WITCH

Silence, fool. I know the law. What I say I saw, I saw. What I saw . . .

JESTER

She's on a seesaw. I saw, you saw; he saw, she saw.

MAIDENS

On a seesaw, on a seesaw. I saw, you saw, he saw, she saw.

PRINCESS

What she tells us may be true. And if it is, what can we do?

JESTER

If you ask me, we should listen to the lad who did the kissin'.

WITCH

I object. It would not be wise. He would only tell you lies.

PRINCESS SARA

Let him speak. Come, lad, this way. Now then, what have you to say?

GEOFFREY

Please, your highness. I confess, when I saw such loveliness, it was too much to resist. I just thought she should be kissed. So I kissed her, kissed her twice. It was very, very nice.

JESTER

So he kissed her, kissed her twice. It was very, very nice.

WITCH

There, you see, he broke the law. What I say I saw, I saw.

JESTER

Please don't start all that again.

WITCH

But he stole a kiss, that's plain.

PRINCESS

Yes. It looks as if it's true, and I'll have to punish you.

MISS ROSE

No, please, let me say a word. It is not the way you heard. Please, he did not steal the kiss, I gave it to him just like this.

Rose kisses Geoffrey.

JESTER

There, you see, I had a feeling this was not a case of stealing.

PRINCESS SARA

I'm not sure. It's not quite plain. Could I see that kiss again?

Geoffrey and Miss Rose kiss again.

PRINCESS SARA

You were right. I have a feeling this was not a case of stealing.

VIZIER

Right. The law has been abused. This lad has falsely been accused.

JESTER

He is hers and she is his'n. That old witch should go to prison.

PRINCESS

You are a very wicked woman.

WITCH

Princess, I am only human.

MALE SPEAKER

Listen to the old grandmommy.

(to the witch)

You are a nasty peeping tommy.

PRINCESS

Banish her from here forever. Never show your face here, never.

MALES AND FEMALES

Banish her from here forever. Never show your face here, never.

The witch is hauled off, protesting.

WITCH

What I say, I saw, I saw. I know my rights. I know the law.

PRINCESS SARA

(to Miss Rose)

Come and sit beside me here. Your kiss has made things very clear.

MISS ROSE

Thank you, princess.

PRINCESS

Don't thank me; it was that kiss that set you free.

JESTER

Now we are through with this arraignment, let us have
some entertainment.

PRINCESS

Bring the dancers, bring the singers. Bring the good
old working ringers.

Fanfare. A troupe of ballerinas come in and dance. They hud-
dle, and out of the midst comes Sara, dressed as a ballerina.
She dances with the other ballerinas.

VIZIER

The new ballerina, she pleases you?

PRINCESS SARA

She's a very good dancer. She looks familiar too.

The ballerina Sara continues to dance with the troupe until
they finish.

Sara is awakened from her dream by Ram Dass rapping on her
window.

SARA CREWE

A nice dream. I feel quite warm. I don't want to wake
up. I haven't waked up.

Sara gets up and sees an array of food at a candlelit table and
a fire in the fireplace. Two satin robes are draped over the foot
of her bed. Two pairs of furry slippers are on the floor.

SARA

I must be dreaming. I'm dreaming. I must be dreaming, for it feels warm.

Sara knocks on Becky's door, which leads into Sara's room.

SARA

Becky. Becky, come quick. Becky. Becky.

Becky comes in.

BECKY

Yes, Miss.

SARA CREWE

Oh, Becky, look.

BECKY

Oh no, Miss, do you see what I do?

SARA CREWE

I don't know what you see. I don't think I believe what I'm seeing.

BECKY

Well, I never.

SARA CREW

Have you seen that?

BECKY

Yes, Miss.

SARA CREWE

What do you see?

BECKY

Oh, I see a fire, Miss.

SARA CREWE

And a table with food on it and a rug and a lamp and slippers.

BECKY

I do indeed, Miss. How did it all get here? Did you pretend it into happening?

SARA CREWE

I don't know. I never pretended as good as this before. Look at these.

She goes over and picks up a satin robe.
Ram Dass and Lord Wickham look over from the next window.

RAM DASS

If the little Missy Sahib knew, she would be over here to thank you.

LORD WICKHAM

I don't want them to know. Who wants any thanks?

Back in Sara's room:

BECKY

Oh, Miss, you're beautiful.

SARA CREWE

Thank you, Becky.

Sara drapes another robe over Becky.

SARA

Now let's try this one on you. Isn't it beautiful?

BECKY

Oh yes, Miss.

SARA CREWE

It's perfect. And real satin too. Let's try the slippers and see if they're real. Do they feel like slippers to you?

BECKY

They feel soft and warm.

SARA CREWE

This feels soft and warm too. They're as real as we are. I don't believe it's a dream after all.

BECKY

You suppose the food is real, Miss?

They go over to the table.

SARA CREWE

Let's see. I can smell kippers, can you?

Sara lifts a lid from one of the dishes.

BECKY

Kippers, as I live!

Sara pulls a cloth from a bowl.

SARA CREWE

What about this? It's muffins. This tastes like a muffin. Is it one?

BECKY

A muffin if ever was! It must be magic, Miss.

SARA CREWE

And we'd better be quick before it melts away.

They start eating ravenously.

Back in the hospital ward, two doctors enter and go up to Captain Crewe's bed.

DOCTOR 1

What sort of a night did he pass?

NURSE

He rested comfortably, Doctor.

DOCTOR 2

Will we be able to send him with the others?

DOCTOR 1

Oh yes, he'll stand the journey all right. Get him ready to be sent with group D. They'll be leaving about an hour.

NURSE

Very well, Doctor.

Now Sara is bringing a full coal scuttle into Lavinia's room and puts it into the scuttle near the hearth. Lavinia and Jessie are sitting on a settee, eating chocolates.

LAVINIA
(to Sara)

I hear you're being punished.

(to Jessie)

Do you think we ought to offer her a chocolate?

JESSIE

You might let her smell them.

LAVINIA

Ms. Minchin surely couldn't object to that. Would you care to?

SARA CREWE

I don't want to smell them and I don't want to eat them, thank you.

LAVINIA

You don't. Why not?

SARA CREWE

I've had much nicer things than chocolates this morning.

LAVINIA

Listen to the princess, pretending again.

SARA CREWE

I'm not pretending. I had the most wonderful things to eat that anyone ever had.

LAVINIA

Why, you little liar! You haven't even had breakfast.

SARA CREWE

Pardon me, but I really have. And if you will excuse me for saying so, it isn't polite to call people liars.

LAVINIA

How dare you talk back to me!

SARA CREWE

Was I doing that? My goodness.

Sara dumps the ashes from the coal scuttle over Lavinia.

SARA

So sorry.

·LAVINIA
(screaming)

You wait until I tell Mrs. Minchin on you!

Sara comes into her room. Becky is still there.

SARA CREWE

Everything is still here, Becky.

BECKY

Yes, it is.

SARA CREWE

Thank heaven it's stopped raining.

BECKY

Are you going someplace, Miss?

SARA CREWE

To the hospital. Oh, Becky, perhaps everything is going to change for us. Perhaps I'll find my father this time and he'll take us away from here.

The door opens. Miss Minchin comes in.

BECKY

Oh Lord, it's the missus.

MISTRESS AMANDA MINCHIN

Sara, how dare you! What's happened to this room?

SARA CREWE

That's what we would like to know. I woke up this morning, here everything was, even to the food and the fire.

MISTRESS AMANDA MINCHIN

Where did you get these things?

SARA CREWE

I don't know. This is because I dreamed such a beautiful dream last night that it came true.

MISTRESS AMANDA MINCHIN

But these articles are rare and costly. You stole them, didn't you?

SARA CREWE

Oh, no. Miss Minchin, we didn't take these things.

MISTRESS AMANDA MINCHIN

I'll give you one more chance to tell me the truth.

SARA CREWE

But I am telling you the truth. They just came.

BECKY

They did indeed, ma'am.

MISTRESS AMANDA MINCHIN
(to Becky)

You go to your room.

Becky runs out.

MISTRESS AMANDA MINCHIN

This is a matter for the police.

SARA CREWE

Oh, please, Miss Minchin, please don't call the police.

MISTRESS AMANDA MINCHIN

Of course I'll call them.

SARA CREWE

Oh, Miss Minchin!

Miss Minchin goes out and locks both Sara's and Becky's doors. Becky comes into Sara's room through the door that connects the two rooms.

BECKY

We are prisoners now, sure enough, Miss, and the police coming too.

SARA CREWE

I can't be arrested. Those new wounded men are at the hospital, and I've got to get there.

BECKY

I don't see how you can. And us locked us in!

SARA CREWE

Come, Becky, quick.

BECKY

Where are we going, Miss?

SARA CREWE

Follow me.

They go out on to the balcony and cross over the ledge to Lord Wickham's window.

BECKY

Oh, I'm frightened, Miss.

SARA CREWE

I'm frightened too, this time, Becky. Come on, give me your hand.

They are now on Lord Wickham's ledge. Becky looks down fearfully at the space below.

BECKY

Oh, no, Miss.

SARA CREWE

Don't be afraid, Becky.

Sara raps on the window repeatedly. Ram Dass comes to the window and opens it.

RAM DASS

Ah. What game is this, little Missy Sahib?

SARA CREWE

May we please go through your house? We're running away from the police.

RAM DASS

And a very nice game too. Will you enter?

SARA

We'd like to very much indeed.

Ram Dass helps them both in. They go in and down the stairs of Lord Wickham's house.

You seem in great haste, Missy Sahib. Could you not stop for a cup of tea?

Sara drops her wrap. Ram Dass picks it up for her.

SARA CREWE

Oh, thank you. We're in too big a hurry.

RAM DASS

I see. Still playing the game of the police. I hope you escape them safely, Missy Sahib.

SARA CREWE

Oh, why?

BECKY

Oh, no!

They go out Lord Wickham's front door. As they do, Miss Minchin exits her door with a policeman.

MISTRESS AMANDA MINCHIN

There they are. Stop them.

SARA CREWE

Oh, Becky, run, run!

MISTRESS AMANDA MINCHIN

Sara, Becky, stop where you are. Becky, Sara!

The girls run; Becky falls.

MISTRESS AMANDA MINCHIN

Go after the other one. I'll take care of her.

Sara still runs on.

SARA CREWE

Watch out, Becky, don't slip.

Sara looks behind her and sees that Becky has fallen.

SARA

Becky, where are you?

Sara runs on. The policeman goes after her, but slips and nearly falls himself. Sara hides by running alongside a large wagon.

In front of Miss Minchin's house:

MISTRESS AMANDA MINCHIN

Becky, you little thief. You'll go to jail for this. Both of you.

BECKY

You'll never catch her. Mr. Bertie will see to that.

A maid comes out of Miss Minchin's house.

MAID

So that's where she's gone. Oh, did you find her, ma'am?

MISTRESS AMANDA MINCHIN

Take this little thief, and don't let her out your sight until I return.

The maid takes Becky inside. Miss Minchin goes out and sees the policeman, who has come back.

MISTRESS AMANDA MINCHIN

Didn't you catch her?

POLICEMAN

She got away in the traffic, ma'am. I couldn't find her anywhere. Do you know where she's likely to be?

MISTRESS AMANDA MINCHIN

I do. Cabby!

A cab halts.

CABBY

Whoa.

Miss Minchin and the policeman get in the cab.

MISTRESS AMANDA MINCHIN

Harvard Hospital, and hurry, please.

In the hospital ward, Captain Crewe is sitting in a wheelchair, with a bandage around his head. Two nurses are attending him.

CAPTAIN REGINALD CREWE

Sara. Sara.

NURSE

He never stops calling for her.

Outside, Sara rushes through a large throng, which is gathered in front of the hospital. She reaches the foot of the hospital steps, which are being guarded by a policeman.

POLICEMAN

Step aside a little bit, will you? Thanks.

The policeman sees Sara and stops her.

POLICEMAN

You can't go in there. No visitors allowed for an hour.

SARA CREWE

But that might be too late.

POLICEMAN

Run along, little girl, will you? There's a good little girl.

Sara goes off a short distance. The policeman addresses another man in front of him.

POLICEMAN

I'm sorry, sir. No visitors allowed for an hour.

MALE SPEAKER

But we must go in.

POLICEMAN

Sorry, sir. You can stand over there if that's all right.

While the policeman is thus occupied, Sara runs up the stairs behind him.

Sara runs through the entrance hall of the hospital. A nurse is passing by an officer, who is standing at the foot of the stairs.

NURSE

Have you seen Captain Marks?

ARMY OFFICER

I believe he just went through the hall, Miss.

Sara runs upstairs. The army officer stops her.

ARMY OFFICER

Sorry, young one, you can't go upstairs now.

SARA CREWE

I've got to. I've got to see if my father's here before Miss
Minchin catches me.

ARMY OFFICER

Now, run along, do as you're told.

Sara goes down the stairs, then backtracks and runs up the
stairs fast.

ARMY OFFICER

I say, come back here. You can't go up there.

The army officer runs up the stairs after her.

ARMY OFFICER

You know you can be in trouble! All right. Come back
here.

She runs through the upstairs corridor; the officer runs after
her. He catches her coming into one of the wards.

ARMY OFFICER

You can't come in here. You can't come in here.

SARA CREWE

Let me go. Let me go. I want to be here. I will, I will.

The ward is full of high-ranking officers surrounding the aged
Queen Victoria, who is sitting in a wheelchair, visiting a patient.

QUEEN VICTORIA

What is it the child wants?

SARA CREWE

Oh, please, please don't let him take me away.

QUEEN VICTORIA

What is it, child?

SARA CREWE

My father, they said he was killed Mafeking, but I don't believe it. Maybe he's with the new wounded men. They won't let me look. And if they don't, perhaps I'll never have another chance. Can you make them let me look?

QUEEN VICTORIA

Colonel, will you please see that this child is escorted through the wards?

COLONEL

With your permission, I shall accompany her personally, Your Majesty.

SARA CREWE

(to the queen)

What is your name?

QUEEN VICTORIA

Victoria. What is yours?

SARA CREWE

Sara. Oh, Your Majesty!

She bends down and kisses the queen's hand.

QUEEN VICTORIA

Colonel! I hope you'll find your father, my dear. A thorough search, Colonel.

SARA CREWE

Oh, thank you, Your Majesty.

QUEEN VICTORIA

Goodbye, my dear.

SARA CREWE

Goodbye.

The assembled, including the queen, look after her with concern. In the hospital hallway:

COLONEL

Have you been through any of the wards yet?

SARA CREWE

Every day, sir.

An orderly wheels out Captain Crewe in a wheelchair. But the backs of the Colonel and Sara are turned, and they do not see him. He is wheeled off, still looking absent. The Colonel and Sara go off to another corridor.

COLONEL

I think we'd better cover this wing first.

They go into a hospital ward.

COLONEL

We are searching for a patient.

NURSE

Yes, sir.

COLONEL

Go right along, dear.

Sara goes off to look at a patient. We see Geoffrey in a bed, with his hand in a bandage, and Miss Rose, who is tending him and gives him a glass of water. But they are screened off from Sara, and she does not see them.

ROSE

All right?

GEOFFREY HAMILTON

Thank you, darling.

Sara comes from behind the screen and sees them now.

SARA CREWE

Miss Rose!

ROSE

Sara, darling!

GEOFFREY HAMILTON

Sara!

SARA CREWE

Oh, Mr. Geoffrey. You're home. You're back again. Now you can tell me where my daddy is.

ROSE

Well, Geoffrey didn't get as far as Mafeking, dear.

SARA CREWE

Then you don't know. You didn't even see it?

GEOFFREY HAMILTON

No dear. I didn't. I'm sorry.

The Colonel approaches.

COLONEL

Have you found him?

SARA CREW

Oh no, sir. This is my friend Mr. Geoffrey and his wife.
Mr. & Mrs. Hamilton.

COLONEL

How'd you do?

SARA CREWE

I'm afraid I can't introduce you, because I don't know
your name.

COLONEL GORDON

Colonel Gordon.

SARA CREWE

This is Colonel Gordon. He's helping me to search the
hospital.

Geoffrey is about to sit up.

COLONEL GORDON
(to Geoffrey)

Don't bother.

GEOFFREY HAMILTON

How do you do, sir?

COLONEL GORDON

I'm very happy to know you both. From Mafeking?

GEOFFREY HAMILTON

No sir. An army mule and a British mule at that.

COLONEL GORDON
(laughing)

That's adding insult to injury.

A nurse approaches.

NURSE

Sorry, sir. It's time for the patient's drops.

GEOFFREY HAMILTON

I'd rather face that mule.

SARA CREWE

I'll come back later, Miss Rose, just as soon as I've gone through the other wards.

ROSE

I'll wait for you, dear.

COLONEL GORDON

Goodbye.

ROSE

Goodbye.

GEOFFREY HAMILTON

Goodbye. Goodbye, sir. Be sure to come back, Sara.

SARA CREWE

I will.

Sara leaves. Geoffrey and Rose look after her.

GEOFFREY HAMILTON

Poor little thing. She'll never stop hoping.

Outside the hospital, Miss Minchin is arguing with a sergeant. A policeman is standing next to them.

MISTRESS AMANDA MINCHIN

I insist that you send for my brother.

SERGEANT

Very well, ma'am. But you can't get in, brother or no brother.

The sergeant goes into the hospital.

MISTRESS AMANDA MINCHIN

We will get in. My brother will see to that.

POLICEMAN

I hope you're right, Ma'am.

In a hospital corridor, men are being carried out on stretchers, directed by an officer. Captain Crewe is being wheeled out in his wheelchair by an orderly. A nurse is accompanying them.

OFFICER

All filled now. This man *(Captain Crewe)* will have to wait for the next ambulance.

ORDERLY

Alright. I think you'd better take him into the waiting room. These halls are much too drafty.

ORDERLY

I think I'd better.

The orderly wheels Captain Crewe into a ward. Sara and Colonel Gordon come out of another ward.

COLONEL GORDON

I am very sorry you couldn't find your father.

SARA CREWE

Thank you just the same, sir.

COLONEL GORDON

He may be on the next convoy of wounded; I wouldn't give up hope.

SARA CREWE

I won't, sir.

COLONEL GORDON

Goodbye, and God bless.

SARA CREWE

Goodbye.

Sara hears the voice of Miss Minchin offscreen, shouting at Bertie.

MISTRESS AMANDA MINCHIN

I know that they were stolen!

Sara rushes into the same ward that Captain Crewe has just been wheeled in to. Miss Minchin, Bertie, and the policeman enter the corridor.

HUBERT "BERTIE" MINCHIN

Sara steal? Preposterous!

MISTRESS AMANDA MINCHIN

I have proof. I intend to turn her over to the authorities. She's in this hospital, and I intend to find her.

HUBERT "BERTIE" MINCHIN

Now, look here, you . . .

MISTRESS AMANDA MINCHIN

I insist that every room be searched.

Sara is now in the same room as her father, listening at the door. He is in his wheelchair, turned away from her, and she does not see him.. Sara opens the door cautiously to see if the way is clear.

CAPTAIN REGINALD CREWE
(muttering)

Sara. Sara.

SARA CREWE

Daddy?

CAPTAIN REGINALD CREWE
(absently)

Sara.

Sara turns and sees Captain Crewe. She closes the door and runs to him.

SARA CREWE

Daddy. Oh, Daddy. It is you. I found you. I found you. They said you were dead. But I knew you weren't. I knew you'd come back. Oh, Daddy, hold me, hold me close. You won't ever go away again, will you? Will you, Daddy? What's the matter, Daddy? Why don't you talk to me?

Captain Crewe still does not recognize her.

CAPTAIN REGINALD CREWE

Sara?

SARA CREWE

Don't you know me, Daddy? I'm Sara. I'm Sara.

CAPTAIN REGINALD CREWE

Sara. Where is my daughter?

SARA CREWE

Oh, Daddy, something's happened to you. Mr. Bertie, Mr. Bertie! Oh, Daddy, you've got to know me. Look at me. Look at me.

(sobbing)

Oh, Daddy.

CAPTAIN REGINALD CREWE

(absently)

You mustn't cry. You mustn't cry. We must be good soldiers, you know?

SARA CREWE

But I have been a good soldier, Daddy, and you don't know me.

CAPTAIN REGINALD CREWE

My little Sara never cried.

SARA CREW

But I'm Sara. I'm Sara.

Captain Crewe looks at her. His mind clears, and he recognizes her.

CAPTAIN REGINALD CREWE

Yes! Yes! Sara. Sara, my baby.

SARA CREWE

Oh, Daddy, you . . .

CAPTAIN REGINALD CREWE

My Sara, my darling, my baby, Sara. Sara. Sara, my darling.

They kiss and hug ardently.

Outside in the corridor, Bertie is arguing with Amanda, the policeman standing by.

HUBERT "BERTIE" MINCHIN

Oh, don't be ridiculous, Amanda.

MISTRESS AMANDA MINCHIN

Then how do you account for those robes and other things that are there?

HUBERT "BERTIE" MINCHIN

Perhaps a little bird brought them in. Perhaps they grew legs and walked in. I don't know. All I do know is that little Sara wouldn't steal.

An orderly runs up to Bertie.

ARMY OFFICER

Bertie?

HUBERT "BERTIE" MINCHIN

Yes.

ARMY OFFICER

Bertie, what do you think has happened? The little princess has found her father.

HUBERT "BERTIE" MINCHIN

She's found him?

MISTRESS AMANDA MINCHIN

Captain Crewe is alive?

HUBERT "BERTIE" MINCHIN

Of course he's alive. How could she find him if he wasn't alive?

Captain Crewe is being wheeled down the corridor by an orderly, attended by a nurse and Sara. She sees Bertie.

SARA CREWE

Oh, Mr. Bertie, I found my father.

HUBERT "BERTIE" MINCHIN

Darling, I'm so glad.

Queen Victoria is also being wheeled by in her wheelchair. She nods to Sara Crewe. All salute, including Captain Crewe, who stands up from his wheelchair. Sara salutes too.

SARA CREWE
(whispering to the queen)

My daddy!

The queen smiles back at her.

THE END

www.ingramcontent.com/pod-product-compliance
Lightning Source LLC
Chambersburg PA
CBHW061321120726
48001CB00002B/619